SELFIE CARE

6 Healthy Habits to Boost Your Energy and Mood!

Written by
Casey Pehrson, Ed.S.

Illustrated by
Antalyaa Khan

"**Hi Gus!**" Jake exclaimed. "**Are you having a great day?**"

"**Um, not really,**" Gus replied. "**It has only been okay.**"

"**It's nice and sunny,**" Jake observed. "**Want to go ride bikes outside?**"

"**I don't feel like it,**" Gus answered. "**How about another time.**"

01

"**Let's play catch!**" Jake suggested, while holding up his new football.

"**Not today,**" Gus murmured in reply. "**I don't feel like that at all.**"

"**Want to build a fort?**" Jake proposed. "**We could put blankets on the stairs!**"

"**I don't feel like it,**" Gus declined, as he plopped down on a chair.

"Let's play a game!" Jake recommended. "Doesn't that sound like it'd be fun?"

"Um, not really," answered Gus. "Last time we played a game, you won."

"Let's play again!" Jake expressed. "Maybe you'll win this round we play!"

"I don't feel like it," Gus responded. "How about another day."

"Do you want a snack?" Jake offered. **"Does fruit sound good to eat?**
My mom just picked some peaches, and they're really, really sweet!"
"I don't feel like it," Gus refused, as he stood and shook his head.
"I think I'll have some candy and a soda pop instead."

"**What do you think?**" Jake asked, politely. "**Is there something you'd like to do?**"
"**Don't ask me,**" Gus answered back to him. "**I haven't got a clue.**"
"**Well, see you later,**" Jake waved goodbye. "**Maybe we can play another day?**"
"**I won't feel like it,**" Gus responded, as Jake turned and walked away.

Several weeks went by and all of Gus's days were filled with gloom,
His free time was spent playing video games and eating candy in his room.
As Gus sat alone, it dawned on him: **"Wow, this really stinks!
My energy and mood are low—I don't feel like doing anything!"**

Gus thought to himself, **"My friend Jake is really fun to be around,**
He always seems so happy, like nothing gets him down.
Whenever Jake is in the room, he always looks so bright,
I'm not sure what he's doing, but he's doing something right!"

Gus looked forward to seeing Jake again to approach him with a question,
He was ready for some input and open to suggestion.
The next day when it was time for school, Gus really wanted to go,
He walked right up to Jake because he couldn't wait to know...

"Will you tell me?" Gus requested. "Because I've been watching you,
And you always seem to have an awesome attitude and mood!
What's your secret? Where do you get all of your energy and spunk?
Because I'm always exhausted and kind of in a funk."

"I'm sorry you've felt so low," said Jake. "But I'll tell you what to do,
It isn't a big secret—you can do these six things too!
It's a pretty simple checklist, I think that you'll agree,
Just one word to keep in mind, and that one word is SELFIE!"

"A selfie?" questioned Gus. "Like a picture with your phone?"
"Not that selfie," Jake explained. "This is a very different one.
This SELFIE is an acronym, so each letter stands for a word,
And when you do these things we'll talk about, you will feel superb!"

SELFIE

SLEEP

The "S" stands for **SLEEP**, and we all need quite a bit,
In order to get enough, you have to prioritize and commit!
Your brain and body go to work when you're asleep at night,
And after a good night's rest, you'll wake up and feel just right!

EXERCISE

The **"E"** is for **EXERCISE**—we all need to work our muscles,
Ride your bike, shoot some hoops, or go for a walk and really hustle!
Your body will reward you when you move and work up a sweat—
You will feel fantastic with the endorphins that you get!

L IGHT

The "L" stands for **LIGHT**, which we all really need,
Because being in the sun activates a thing called Vitamin D.
Fifteen minutes in the sun helps that Vitamin D awake,
Just make sure to put on sunscreen, or else your skin will bake!

FUN

The "F" stands for **FUN**—we all need to take some time,
To kick back and enjoy instead of stressing all our lives.
Our brains get a refresher when we laugh and when we play,
So make it a routine habit to put some fun in every day!

INTERACTION

The "I" is for **INTERACTION**—we all need each other,
So hug your mom and dad, and play with your sister and brother,
Hanging out with our friends is really good for us too,
Because connecting with other people is one of the best things we can do.

The last **"E"** is for **EATING RIGHT**—you really are what you eat,
So load up on the vegetables, and go easy on the treats,
Whole grains, fruits, veggies, dairy, and healthy meats are all nutritious,
And as an added bonus, they also are delicious!

"That's all six parts of SELFIE," said Jake. **"Our acronym is now complete! Can you remember all six things and then repeat them back to me?"**

"Hmm, let's see," Gus remembered. **"It starts with Sleep, Exercise, and Light, Then Fun and Interaction, and the last E is Eating right!"**

LIGHT

FUN

EXERCISE

INTERACTION

SLEEP

EATING RIGHT

"That's amazing!" Jake declared. "I didn't have to tell you twice!
But in order to make this work the best, let me give you some advice...
Some days you won't feel like doing this stuff, but get up and don't delay,
These six things will make you feel better, so go and do them anyway!"

From that day on, Gus made an effort to keep in mind his **SELFIE** list,
Each evening he thought back to see if anything was missed.
He made a point to **Sleep** and **Exercise** and get out in the **Light**,
He had **Fun** and **Interaction** and made sure he was **Eating right**.

SLEEP · EXERCISE · LIGHT · FUN · INTERACTION · EATING RIGHT

Gus really felt incredible—he saw a difference in his mood,
So he walked over to Jake's house to go express his gratitude.
"Thank you, Jake!" Gus said, excitedly. **"I have such awesome energy!
And I know it's all because I'm taking care of my SELFIE!"**

26

SLEEP

Proper sleep is a brain detox, flushing out neural waste that has accumulated during the day.

EXERCISE

Physical exercise releases endorphins, promoting feelings of happiness and well-being.

LIGHT

Sunlight exposure activates Vitamin D for bone, muscle, brain, and immune system health.

FUN

Fun and relaxation lower stress chemicals and cool down an overheated brain.

INTERACTION

Social interaction releases oxytocin, a bonding hormone that fosters feelings of connection.

EATING RIGHT

Good nutrition provides vitamins and minerals for optimal physical functioning.

About **Casey Pehrson, Ed.S.**

- WRITER / AUTHOR

Casey Pehrson has been working in school-based mental health since 2007. After reading dozens of books on depression, and based on years of experience counseling teenagers as a school psychologist, Casey developed "The SELFIE Method" in 2017. The simplicity and practicality of the acronym caught on, and she has been giving a popular presentation on the subject ever since. Casey earned her graduate degree from Brigham Young University in 2011, and she currently resides in Utah. As a native of Kansas City, she is an avid sports fan, particularly of her hometown KC teams (go Chiefs!).

1st EDITION 2023

About **Antalyaa Khan**

- ILLUSTRATOR / DESIGNER

Antalyaa Khan has been working in the graphic design industry since 2007, and she has helped individuals and businesses bring their ideas to life through character illustration, infographics, logos, magazines, postcards, flyers, brochures, and website design and development. Known for her attention to detail and skilled use of color, her beautiful, elegant illustrations and designs can be found all over the globe. Antalyaa earned her degree in Graphic and Web Designing from Arena Multimedia in Karachi, Pakistan in 2005.

Made in the USA
Las Vegas, NV
22 August 2024